# Ward No. 6

Anton Chekhov

ISBN: 9798321594575

Imprint: Daybreak Studios

# PREFACE

In "Ward No. 6," Anton Chekhov masterfully delves into the complexities of the human psyche against the backdrop of a mental institution. Set within the confines of a remote provincial hospital, Chekhov unravels the intricacies of sanity, insanity, and the fine line that separates the two.

This timeless novella serves as a poignant commentary on the societal constructs that define normalcy and the individual's struggle to maintain autonomy within such constraints. Through his characters, Chekhov exposes the fragility of human perception and the inherent flaws in systems designed to categorize and treat mental illness.

As readers journey through the corridors of Ward No. 6, they are confronted with profound questions about the nature of existence, the limits of compassion, and the consequences of societal neglect. Chekhov's penetrating insight into the human condition transcends the boundaries of time and place, resonating with audiences across generations.

With its richly drawn characters and thought-provoking narrative, "Ward No. 6" stands as a timeless masterpiece, inviting readers to contemplate the intricacies of the human mind and the fundamental truths that bind us all.

# WARD NO. 6

## I

In the hospital yard stands a small wing, surrounded by a whole forest of burdock, nettle, and wild hemp. Its roof is rusty, the chimney half collapsed, the steps to the porch rotted and overgrown with grass, and only traces of plaster remain on the walls. Its front faces the hospital, while its back overlooks the fields, separated by a gray hospital fence with nails. These nails, pointing upwards, along with the fence and the wing itself, have that special dismal, ominous look that we only see in hospital and prison buildings.

If you're not afraid of getting stung by nettles, come along the narrow path leading to the wing, and let's see what's inside. Opening the first door, we enter the porch. Here, near the walls and by the stove, heaps of hospital rubbish are piled up. Mattresses, old worn-out dressing gowns, trousers, shirts with blue stripes, useless, worn-out shoes – all this ragged stuff is piled up, crumpled, tangled, rotting, emitting a suffocating odor.

On the rubbish, always with a pipe in his mouth, lies watchman Nikita, an old retired soldier with faded shoulder straps. He has a stern, weathered face, drooping eyebrows giving him the expression of a steppe watchdog, and a red nose; he's short, lean-looking, but with an imposing posture and huge fists. He belongs to the category of those simple-minded, positive, dutiful, and dull people who love order more than anything else in the world and are convinced that they need to beat others to achieve it. He hits in the face, in the chest, in the back, wherever he can, and firmly believes that without this, there would be no order here.

Next, you enter a large, spacious room, occupying the

entire wing, not counting the porch. The walls here are smeared with dirty blue paint, the ceiling is sooty like in a barn – it's clear that in winter stoves are fired here and there's often smoke. The windows are disfigured from the inside by iron bars. The floor is gray and splintery. It smells of sour cabbage, tallow smoke, bedbugs, and ammonia, and this stench, in the first few minutes, makes you feel as if you're entering a menagerie.

In the room are beds bolted to the floor. On them sit and lie people in blue hospital gowns and old-fashioned caps. These are the insane.

There are five of them here. Only one has a noble title, while the rest are all commoners. Closest to the door, a tall, slender commoner with shiny red mustaches and tearful eyes sits, leaning his head and staring into space. Day and night, he mourns, shaking his head, sighing, and bitterly smiling; he rarely participates in conversations and usually doesn't respond to questions. He eats and drinks mechanically when given. Judging by his agonizing cough, emaciation, and flush on his cheeks, he's beginning to suffer from consumption.

Behind him follows a little, lively, very agile old man with a sharp beard and black, curly hair like that of a Negro. During the day, he walks around the ward from window to window or sits on his bed, cross-legged like a Turk, and tirelessly, like a snow bunting, whistles, quietly sings, and giggles. He displays childlike cheerfulness and liveliness even at night, when he rises to pray to God, which means pounding his chest with fists and poking at the doors with his fingers. This is Moiseyka the Jew, a simpleton who went mad twenty years ago when his cap workshop burned down.

Of all the inhabitants of ward No. 6, only he is allowed to leave the wing and even the hospital yard to go out into the street. He has enjoyed this privilege for a long time, probably as a long-time resident of the hospital and as a quiet, harmless fool, a city fool, whom people have long been accustomed to seeing on the streets surrounded by boys and dogs. In his gown, in a funny cap, and in shoes, sometimes barefoot and even without pants, he walks the streets, stopping at gates and benches, and asks for a penny. In one place, they'll give him kvass, in another – bread, in a third – a penny, so he usually returns to the wing well-fed and rich. Everything he brings with him is taken away from him by Nikita for his own benefit. The soldier does this roughly, with zeal, rummaging through his pockets and calling God as a witness that he will never let the Jew out onto the street again and that disturbances are the worst thing in the world for him.

Moiseyka loves to serve. He brings water to his comrades, covers them when they sleep, promises each one to bring back a penny from the street and to sew a new cap for them; he even feeds his neighbor on the left, a paralytic, with a spoon. He does this not out of compassion or any humane considerations, but by imitating and involuntarily submitting to his neighbor on the right, Gromov.

Ivan Dmitrievich Gromov, a man of thirty-three, of noble birth, a former judicial officer and provincial secretary, suffers from persecution mania. He either lies curled up in bed or walks from corner to corner, as if for exercise, but rarely sits. He is always agitated, excited, and tense with some vague, undefined expectation. The slightest noise in the porch or a shout outside is enough to make him raise his head and listen: aren't they coming for him? Aren't they looking for him? And his face at this moment expresses extreme anxiety and disgust.

I like his wide, bony face, always pale and unhappy, reflecting like a mirror the tormented struggle and prolonged fear of his soul. His grimaces are strange and painful, but the delicate features, marked on his face by deep and sincere suffering, are rational and intelligent, and his eyes have a warm, healthy glow. I like him himself, polite, courteous, and unusually delicate in dealing with everyone except Nikita. When someone drops a button or a spoon, he quickly jumps out of bed and picks it up. Every morning, he wishes his comrades a good morning, and when he goes to bed, he wishes them a good night.

In addition to his constantly tense state and grimacing, his madness manifests itself in the following way. Sometimes in the evenings, he wraps himself in his gown and, shaking all over, chattering his teeth, he starts walking quickly from corner to corner and between the beds. It looks as if he has a high fever. By the way he suddenly stops and looks at his comrades, it's clear that he wants to say something very important, but apparently realizing that they won't listen or won't understand, he impatiently shakes his head and continues to walk. But soon the desire to speak prevails over all considerations, and he gives himself free rein and speaks fervently and passionately. His speech is disorderly, feverish, like delirium, impulsive and not always understandable, but in it, you can hear, in both words and voice, something extremely good. When he speaks, you recognize in him both a madman and a man. It's difficult to convey on paper his insane speech. He talks about human wickedness, about violence that tramples truth, about the beautiful life that will come on earth over time, about the window grilles that remind him every minute of the stupidity and cruelty of the oppressors. It turns out to be a disorderly, incongruous potpourri of old but not yet finished songs.

II

Twelve to fifteen years ago, in the city, on the main street, in their own house lived the official Gromov, a respectable and well-to-do man. He had two sons: Sergey and Ivan. Sergey, already a fourth-year university student, fell ill with galloping consumption and died, and this death seemed to mark the beginning of a series of misfortunes that suddenly befell the Gromov family. A week after Sergey's funeral, the old father was brought to trial for forgeries and embezzlement and soon died in the prison hospital from typhus. The house and all the movable property were sold at auction, leaving Ivan Dmitrievich and his mother with nothing.

Previously, while his father was alive, Ivan Dmitrievich, living in St. Petersburg, where he studied at the university, received sixty to seventy rubles a month and had no idea of need. But now he had to drastically change his life. He had to give penny lessons from morning till night, engage in correspondence, and still go hungry, as all his earnings were sent to his mother for sustenance. Ivan Dmitrievich could not endure such a life; he lost heart, wasted away, and, abandoning the university, went home. Here, in the town, he obtained a position as a teacher at the district school through connections, but he did not get along with his colleagues, did not appeal to the students, and soon left the position. His mother died. For six months he wandered without a job, subsisting only on bread and water, then he became a judicial officer. He held this position until he was dismissed due to illness.

Even in his youthful student years, he never appeared healthy. He was always pale, thin, prone to colds, ate little, and slept poorly. A single glass of wine made him dizzy and caused hysteria. He always felt drawn to people, but due to his irritable character and suspiciousness, he did not get close to anyone and had no friends. He always spoke of townspeople with disdain, saying that their coarse ignorance and sleepy animal life seemed disgusting and repulsive to him. He spoke in a tenor voice, loudly, passionately, either disapprovingly and indignantly or with enthusiasm and amazement, and always sincerely. Whatever the topic of conversation, he always brought it back to one thing: it was stifling and dull to live in the town, society lacked higher interests, leading a dull, meaningless life, diversifying it with violence, gross debauchery, and hypocrisy; scoundrels were well-fed and dressed, while the honest ones ate scraps; schools were needed, a local newspaper with honest direction, a theater, public readings, unity of intellectual forces; society needed to recognize itself and be horrified. In his judgments of people, he painted with thick strokes, only in black and white, recognizing no shades; humanity was divided for him into honest people and scoundrels; there was no middle ground. He always spoke passionately and enthusiastically about women and love, but he was never in love.

Despite the sharpness of his judgments and his nervousness, he was loved in the town and affectionately called Vaney behind his back. His innate delicacy, helpfulness, integrity, moral purity, his worn-out coat, sickly appearance, and family misfortunes inspired good, warm, and sad feelings; besides, he was well-educated and well-read, knew, according to townspeople, everything, and was something like a walking encyclopedia in the town.

He read a lot. Sometimes he would sit in the club, nervously twirling his beard and flipping through magazines and books; and from his face, it was evident that he was not reading but devouring, barely chewing. Apparently, reading was one of his unhealthy habits, as he attacked everything that came his way with the same greed, even last year's newspapers and calendars. At home, he always read lying down.

III

One autumn morning, raising the collar of his coat and splashing through the mud, through alleys and backyards, Ivan Dmitrievich made his way to a bourgeois's house to collect on an execution order. His mood was gloomy, as it always was in the mornings. In one of the alleys, he encountered two prisoners in shackles, accompanied by four armed guards. Ivan Dmitrievich had often encountered prisoners before, and each time they aroused feelings of compassion and awkwardness in him, but this meeting now left him with a peculiar, strange impression. Suddenly, for some reason, it seemed to him that he too could be put in

6

shackles and led through the mud to prison in the same way. After visiting the bourgeois and returning home, he met a familiar police supervisor near the post office, who greeted him and walked a few steps with him along the street, and for some reason, this seemed suspicious to him. All day at home, he couldn't get the prisoners and soldiers with rifles out of his head, and an inexplicable sense of unease prevented him from reading and concentrating. In the evening, he didn't light a fire at home, and at night, he couldn't sleep, constantly thinking that he might be arrested, shackled, and thrown into prison. He didn't know of any guilt on his part and could vouch that he would never kill, set fire, or steal, not now or in the future, but couldn't a crime be committed accidentally, involuntarily? Couldn't there be slander, or worse, a judicial error? After all, the centuries-old popular experience teaches not to swear off the prison before the sum and the prison itself. And with the current state of the judiciary, a judicial error is very possible, and there's nothing mysterious about it. People who have official or business relations with others' suffering, such as judges, police officers, doctors, with time and habit, harden to such an extent that they would like, but cannot treat their clients other than formally; from this perspective, they are no different from the peasant who slaughters sheep and calves in the backyards without noticing the blood. But with a formal, soulless attitude towards the individual, in order to deprive an innocent person of all rights and sentence them to hard labor, a judge needs only one thing: time. Just time to observe some formalities for which the judge is paid a salary, and then it's all over. And then try to find justice and protection in this small, dirty town, two hundred versts from the railroad! And is it not ridiculous to think about justice when any violence is justified by society as reasonable and expedient necessity, and any act of mercy, for example, an acquittal, provokes a whole explosion of unsatisfied, vengeful feeling?

In the morning, Ivan Dmitrievich woke up in horror,

with cold sweat on his forehead, already fully convinced that he could be arrested at any moment. If yesterday's heavy thoughts didn't leave him for so long, he thought, then there must be some truth to them. Could they really have come to mind without any reason? The constable walked past the windows unhurriedly: it was not for nothing. Here, two people stopped near the house and remained silent. Why were they silent?

For Ivan Dmitrievich, agonizing days and nights followed. Everyone passing by the windows or entering the courtyard seemed like spies and detectives to him. At noon, the supervisor usually rode past the street in a carriage; he was returning from his country estate to the police department, but each time Ivan Dmitrievich felt that he was driving too fast and with a special expression – evidently, he was hurrying to announce that a very important criminal had appeared in the city. Ivan Dmitrievich flinched at every ring and knock at the gate, agonized when he met new people at his landlady's; when meeting with policemen and gendarmes, he smiled and whistled to appear indifferent. He didn't sleep all night, waiting for arrest, but snored loudly and sighed, pretending to be asleep, so that his landlady would think he was asleep; after all, if he wasn't sleeping, then his conscience must be troubled – what evidence! Facts and sound logic convinced him that all these fears were nonsense and psychopathy, that there was nothing really terrifying about arrest and prison, if you looked at it more broadly – if only his conscience were calm; but the smarter and more logical he reasoned, the stronger and more painful the spiritual distress became. It was like a hermit trying to clear a spot for himself in a virgin forest; the harder he worked with an ax, the thicker and stronger the forest grew. In the end, seeing that it was useless, Ivan Dmitrievich completely stopped reasoning and surrendered entirely to despair and fear.

He began to isolate himself and avoid people. The service had been distasteful to him before, but now it became unbearable. He was afraid that he might be tricked somehow, that a bribe might be secretly placed in his pocket and then he would be caught, or that he might accidentally make a mistake in the government papers, equivalent to forgery, or lose someone else's money. Strangely enough, at no other time was his thinking as flexible and inventive as it was now, when every day he invented thousands of reasons to seriously fear for his freedom and honor. But at the same time, his interest in the outside world, especially in books, waned significantly, and his memory began to change greatly.

In spring, when the snow melted, two half-decomposed bodies – an old woman and a boy – were found in a ravine near the cemetery, showing signs of violent death. The town was abuzz with talk of these bodies and the unknown killers. Ivan Dmitrievich, to avoid suspicion of being the murderer, walked the streets smiling, but when he met acquaintances, he would pale, blush, and start insisting that there is no greater crime than killing the weak and defenseless. But this lie soon wearied him, and after some reflection, he decided that the best thing for him to do in his situation was to hide in his landlady's cellar. He spent a day in the cellar, then a night, and another day, growing very cold. Finally, waiting for darkness, he sneaked back to his room, stealthily like a thief. He stood in the middle of the room until dawn, motionless and listening intently. Early in the morning, before sunrise, the chimney sweeps came to the landlady's house. Ivan Dmitrievich knew well that they had come to repair the stove in the kitchen, but fear told him that they were policemen disguised as chimney sweeps. He quietly slipped out of the apartment and, seized by terror, ran down the street without his hat and coat. Dogs chased after him, someone shouted behind him, the air whistled in his ears, and Ivan Dmitrievich felt as if all the violence in the world had gathered behind him and was pursuing him.

He was detained, brought home, and the landlady was sent for the doctor. Doctor Andrei Efimych, whom we'll speak of later, prescribed cold compresses for his head and drops of bay leaf, sadly shook his head, and left, telling the landlady that he wouldn't come again because it's not right to interfere with people going mad. Since there was nothing at home to live on or to treat himself with, Ivan Dmitrievich was soon sent to the hospital and placed in a ward for venereal patients. He couldn't sleep at night, was irritable and disturbed the other patients, and soon, at Andrei Efimych's orders, he was transferred to Ward No. 6.

A year later, the town had completely forgotten about Ivan Dmitrievich, and his books, thrown by the landlady into the sleigh under the shed, were scattered by the boys.

IV

Neighbor to Ivan Dmitrievich on the left side was Moiseyka, a Jew, as I mentioned, while on the right side was a man bloated with fat, almost round, with a dull, entirely meaningless face. This is a motionless, gluttonous, and unclean creature, long having lost the ability to think and feel. An acrid, suffocating stench constantly emanates from him. Nikita, who cleans up after him, beats him terribly, with all his might, sparing not his fists; and the terrible thing is not that he is beaten – one can get used to that – but that this dulled animal doesn't respond to the beatings with a sound, a movement, or a change in the expression of his eyes; he only sways slightly, like a heavy barrel.

The fifth and final inhabitant of Ward No. 6 was a townsman who once worked as a mail sorter, a small, thin blonde with a kind, but somewhat cunning face. Judging by his intelligent, serene eyes, which look clearly and cheerfully, he is intelligent and has some very important and pleasant secret. He keeps something under his pillow and under the mattress, which he doesn't show to anyone, not out of fear of it being taken or stolen, but out of embarrassment. Sometimes he approaches the window, turns his back to his companions, puts something on his chest, and bends his head to look; if you approach him during this time, he will become embarrassed and tear something off his chest. But his secret is easy to guess.

"Congratulate me," he often says to Ivan Dmitrievich, "I've been nominated for the Order of Stanislaus, Second Class with a Star. The Second Class with a Star is usually given to foreigners, but for some reason, they want to make an exception for me," he smiles, shrugging in bewilderment. "I never expected this!"

"I don't understand any of this," Ivan Dmitrievich grumpily declares.

"But you know what I'll achieve sooner or later?" continues the former sorter, squinting his eyes cunningly. "I will definitely receive the Swedish 'Polar Star.' It's an order that's worth the effort. A white cross and a black ribbon. It's very beautiful."

Probably, life is nowhere as monotonous as in the ward. In the morning: the patients, except for the paralytic and the fat man, wash in the vestibule from a large basin and dry themselves with the folds of their robes; then they drink tea from tin mugs brought by Nikita from the main building. Each person gets one mug. At noon, they eat cabbage soup and porridge, and in the evening, they have leftover porridge from lunch for dinner. In between, they lie down, sleep, look out the windows, and wander from corner to corner. And so it goes every day. Even the former sorter talks only about the same orders.

Fresh faces are rarely seen in Ward No. 6. The doctor hasn't admitted any new patients for a long time, and there are few people in the world who enjoy visiting madhouses. Every two months, Semen Lazarich, the barber, comes to the ward. We won't talk about how he cuts the lunatics' hair, how Nikita helps him do it, and how the patients are thrown into confusion every time the drunken, smiling barber appears.

Besides the barber, no one ventures into the ward. The patients are condemned to see only Nikita day after day.

However, recently, a rather strange rumor has spread

through the hospital building.

There is a rumor going around that a doctor has supposedly started visiting Ward No. 6.

## V

Strange rumor!

Doctor Andrei Yefimych Ragin is a remarkable man in his own right. It is said that in his early youth he was very devout and preparing himself for a spiritual career. Upon completing his studies at the gymnasium in 1863, he intended to enter the theological academy, but allegedly his father, a doctor of medicine and surgery, sharply scoffed at him and categorically stated that he would not consider him his son if he became a priest. Whether this is true, I do not know, but Andrei Yefimych himself has admitted on several occasions that he never felt called to medicine or any specialized field of study.

Nevertheless, after completing his studies at the medical faculty, he did not join the priesthood. He did not show any religious fervor, and at the beginning of his medical career, he resembled a man of the cloth as little as he does now.

His appearance is heavy, rough, peasant-like: with his face, beard, flat hair, and sturdy, clumsy build, he resembles an innkeeper on a major road, greedy, unrestrained, and surly. His face is stern, covered with blue veins, his eyes small, his nose red. Despite his tall stature and broad shoulders, he has enormous hands and feet; it seems that one blow from his fist could knock the wind out of you. But his step is quiet, and his gait cautious, stealthy; when encountering someone in a narrow corridor, he always stops first to give way, and in a soft, gentle tenor says, "Sorry!" He has a small swelling on his neck, which prevents him from wearing stiff starched collars, so he always wears a soft linen or calico shirt. Generally, he dresses unprofessionally. He wears the same pair of shoes for ten years, and the new clothes he usually buys at the Jewish shop look just as worn and wrinkled on him as the old ones; he wears the same coat to see patients, have lunch, and visit friends; but this is not out of stinginess, but rather out of complete disregard for his appearance.

When Andrei Yefimych arrived in town to take up his position, the "godly institution" was in terrible condition. It was hard to breathe in the wards, corridors, and hospital yard due to the stench. Male patients, caregivers, and their children slept in the wards with the sick. They complained about the unbearable infestation of cockroaches, bedbugs, and mice. There were only two scalpels and no thermometers for the entire hospital; potatoes were kept in the baths. The superintendent, housekeeper, and orderly extorted from the patients, and stories circulated about the old doctor, Andrei Yefimych's predecessor, alleging that he was secretly selling hospital spirits and had assembled a harem of caregivers and female patients. The city was well aware of these disorders and even exaggerated them, but they took them calmly; some justified them by saying that only townspeople and peasants went to the hospital, and they couldn't be dissatisfied because they lived worse at home than in the hospital; they weren't fed on wheat, after all! Others, in justification, said that it was beyond the power of one city, without the help of the zemstvo, to maintain a good hospital; thank God, at least there was a bad one. And the young zemstvo did not open a clinic in the city or nearby, citing the fact that the city already had its own hospital.

Having inspected the hospital, Andrei Yefimych came to the conclusion that this institution was immoral and highly detrimental to the health of the inhabitants. In his opinion, the smartest thing to do would be to release the patients and close the hospital. However, he reasoned that this would not be enough with just his will alone and that it would be futile; if you drive physical and moral impurity from one place, it will move to another; one must wait for it to dissipate on its own. Moreover, if people established the hospital and tolerate it, then it must be necessary for them; prejudices and all these worldly nuisances and filth are necessary, as over time they are transformed into something useful, like manure into fertile soil. There is nothing good on earth that did not have filth at its source.

Upon assuming his position, Andrei Yefimych seemed quite indifferent to the disorder. He only asked the male patients and caregivers not to spend the night in the wards and installed two cabinets with instruments; however, the superintendent, housekeeper, orderly, and surgical assistant remained in their positions.

Andrei Yefimych greatly values intellect and honesty, but he lacks the character and belief in his own authority to arrange a life of intellect and honesty around him. He positively does not know how to command, forbid, or insist. It seems as if he took a vow never to raise his voice or use imperative mood. It is difficult for him to say "give" or "bring"; when he wants to eat, he hesitantly coughs and says to the cook, "Could I have some tea..." or "I'd like to have lunch." However, it is completely beyond him to tell the superintendent to stop stealing, or to dismiss him, or to abolish this unnecessary parasitic position altogether. When Andrei Yefimych is deceived, flattered, or presented with an obviously fraudulent bill for signature, he blushes like a crayfish and feels guilty, but he still signs the bill; when patients complain to him about hunger or rough caregivers, he gets flustered and guiltily mumbles, "Okay, okay, I'll look into it later... Probably just a misunderstanding..."

At first, Andrei Yefimych worked very diligently. He saw patients every day from morning until lunchtime, performed surgeries, and even practiced midwifery. Ladies said of him that he was attentive and had a keen insight into diseases, especially those of children and women. But over time, the work became noticeably monotonous and obviously useless to him. Today you see thirty patients, and tomorrow, you find thirty-five more, the day after tomorrow, forty, and so on day after day, year after year, and yet the mortality rate in the city does not decrease, and the patients do not stop coming. There is no physical possibility to provide serious assistance to forty incoming patients from morning till lunch, which means inevitably resorting to deception. If twelve thousand incoming patients were received in the reporting year, then, simply reasoning, twelve thousand people were deceived. However, it is also impossible to place seriously ill patients in wards and attend to them according to the rules of science because there are rules but no science; and if you leave philosophy and pedantically follow the rules, as other doctors do, then first and foremost, you need cleanliness and ventilation, not dirt, healthy food, not soup made from smelly sour cabbage, and good assistants, not thieves.

And why interfere with people dying if death is a normal and lawful end for everyone? What if some merchant or bureaucrat lives an extra five or ten years? However, if the purpose of medicine is to alleviate suffering with medicines, then one inevitably asks the question: why alleviate it? Firstly, it is said that suffering leads a person to perfection, and secondly, if humanity really learns to alleviate its suffering with pills and drops, then it will completely abandon religion and philosophy, in which it has so far found not only protection from all troubles but even happiness. Pushkin experienced terrible agonies before his death, poor Heine lay paralyzed for several years; why not let Andrei Yefimych or Matryona Savvishna suffer, whose lives are devoid of meaning and would be completely empty and resemble the life of an amoeba if not for suffering?

Suppressed by such reasoning, Andrei Yefimych lowered his hands and began to visit the hospital less frequently.

VI

His life goes like this. Usually, he gets up at eight in the morning, dresses, and has tea. Then he sits in his office to read or goes to the hospital. Here, in the hospital, in a narrow dark corridor, outpatient patients sit, waiting for examination. Men and caregivers run past them, their boots echoing on the brick floor; thin patients in gowns pass by, dead bodies and dishes with filth are carried, children cry, and a draught blows through. Andrei Yefimych knows that such an environment is agonizing for feverish, consumptive, and generally sensitive patients, but what can you do? In the reception room, he is met by Feldsher Sergey Sergeyich, a small, chubby man with a shaved, clean, puffy face, with soft smooth manners and in a new spacious suit, more resembling a senator than a feldsher. He has a huge practice in the city, wears a white tie, and considers himself more knowledgeable than the doctor, who has no practice at all. In the corner of the reception room stands a large icon in a shrine, with a heavy lampada, next to it is a stand covered in white cloth; on the walls hang portraits of bishops, a view of the Svyatogorsk Monastery, and wreaths of dried cornflowers. Sergey Sergeyich is religious and loves splendor. The icon was set up at his expense; on Sundays, at his command, one of the patients reads aloud an akathist in the reception room, and after the reading, Sergey Sergeyich goes around all the wards with a censer, censing them with incense.

There are many patients, and time is short, so the work is limited to just a short interview and dispensing some medicine like fly ointment or castor oil. Andrei Yefimych sits, resting his cheek on his fist, lost in thought, and mechanically asks questions. Sergey Sergeyich also sits, rubbing his hands and occasionally intervening.

"We suffer and endure need because we do not pray well to the merciful Lord. Yes!"

During the examination, Andrei Yefimych does not perform any operations; he has long since stopped doing them, and the sight of blood unpleasantly agitates him. When he has to open a child's mouth to look into their throat, and the child screams and defends themselves with their little hands, his head starts spinning from the noise in his ears and tears well up in his eyes. He hurries to prescribe medicine and waves his hands for the woman to take the child away quickly.

During the examination, he soon tires of the patients' shyness and confusion, the proximity of the splendid Sergey Sergeyich, the portraits on the walls, and his own questions, which he has been asking for over twenty years. And he leaves, having seen five or six patients. The rest are seen by the Feldsher without him.

With the pleasant thought that, thank God, he no longer has a private practice and that nobody will disturb him, Andrei Yefimych, upon returning home, immediately sits down at his desk in the office and begins to read. He reads a lot and always with great pleasure. Half of his salary goes to buying books, and three out of the six rooms in his apartment are cluttered with books and old magazines. He loves historical and philosophical works the most; as for medicine, he subscribes only to "The Doctor," which he always starts reading from the end. His reading usually continues uninterrupted for several hours, and he does not get tired of it. He reads not as fast and impulsive as Ivan Dmitrich used to read, but slowly, with penetration, often pausing at places he likes or finds incomprehensible. Next to the book, there is always a decanter of vodka, and a pickled cucumber or a pickled apple lies directly on the cloth, without a plate. Every half-hour, without taking his eyes off the book, he pours himself a shot of vodka and drinks it, then, without looking, feels for the cucumber and takes a bite.

At three o'clock, he cautiously approaches the kitchen door, coughs, and says:

"Daryushka, I'd like to have lunch..."

After lunch, which was quite poor and untidy, Andrei Yefimych walks through his rooms, crossing his arms over his chest, and thinks. Four o'clock strikes, then five, and he keeps walking and thinking. Occasionally, the kitchen door creaks, and Daryushka's red, sleepy face appears from it.

"Andrei Yefimych, isn't it time for you to drink beer?" she asks anxiously.

"No, it's not time yet... I'll wait... I'll wait..."

By evening, usually, the postmaster, Mikhail Averyanych, comes, the only person in the whole town whose company is not burdensome for Andrei Yefimych. Mikhail Averyanych was once a very wealthy landowner and served in the cavalry, but he went bankrupt and out of necessity joined the postal service in his old age. He has a brisk, healthy appearance, luxurious gray sideburns, well-bred manners, and a loud pleasant voice. He is kind and sensitive but quick-tempered. When someone at the post office protests, disagrees, or simply starts reasoning, Mikhail Averyanych turns purple, shakes all over, and shouts in a booming voice, "Silence!" so the post office has long had a reputation as a place where it's terrifying to be. Mikhail Averyanych respects and loves Andrei Yefimych for his education and noble soul, but he looks down on other common people, treating them with disdain, as he does with his subordinates.

"And here I am!" he says, entering Andrei Yefimych's place. "Hello, my dear! I hope I'm not bothering you, am I?"

"On the contrary, I'm very glad," the doctor replies. "I'm always glad to see you."

The friends sit down on the sofa in the office and smoke in silence for a while.

"Daryushka, let's have some beer!" Andrei Yefimych says.

They drink the first bottle in silence too: the doctor lost in thought and Mikhail Averyanych with a cheerful, animated look, like a man who has something very interesting to tell. The conversation always starts with the doctor.

"It's such a pity," he says slowly and quietly, shaking his head and not looking into the eyes of his interlocutor (he never looks into people's eyes), "such a deep pity, esteemed Mikhail Averyanych, that in our town there are absolutely no people who can carry on an intelligent and interesting conversation. This is a huge deprivation for us. Even the intelligentsia does not rise above mediocrity; its level of development, I assure you, is no higher than that of the lowest class."

"Absolutely right. I agree."

"You yourself know," the doctor continues quietly and deliberately, "that in this world everything is insignificant and uninteresting except for the highest spiritual manifestations of the human mind. The mind draws a sharp line between the animal and the human, hints at the divinity of the latter, and to some extent even substitutes for it the immortality that does not exist. Based on this, the mind serves as the only possible source of enjoyment. Since we do not see or hear around us the mind, we are deprived of pleasure. True, we have books, but it's not at all like live conversation and communication. If I may make a somewhat unfortunate comparison, books are like musical notes, and conversation is like singing."

"Absolutely right."

There is silence. Daryushka comes out of the kitchen and, with an expression of dull sorrow, holding her cheek in her fist, stops in the doorway to listen.

"Oh!" sighs Mikhail Averyanych. "What we've come to expect from the minds of today!"

And he tells how life was once great, fun, and interesting, how there was a smart intelligentsia in Russia that held high notions of honor and friendship. They lent money without a promissory note, and it was considered shameful not to lend a helping hand to a needy comrade. And what expeditions, adventures, clashes, what comrades, what women! And the Caucasus—what an amazing place! And the wife of one battalion commander, a strange woman, would put on an officer's uniform and ride off into the mountains in the evenings, without a guide. They say she had a romance with some prince in the auls.

"Heavenly Queen, Mother..." sighs Daryushka.

"And how they drank! How they ate! And what desperate liberals there were!"

Andrei Yefimych listens but does not hear; he is thinking about something and sipping beer.

"I often dream about intelligent people and conversations with them," he suddenly says, interrupting Mikhail Averyanych. "My father gave me an excellent education, but under the influence of the ideas of the sixties, he made me become a doctor. I feel that if I hadn't listened to him then, I would now be at the center of intellectual movement. Probably, I would be a member of some faculty. Of course, the mind is not eternal and passing, but you already know why I am inclined towards it. Life is a vexing trap. When a thinking person reaches maturity and comes to a mature consciousness, he involuntarily feels as if he is in a trap, from which there is no escape. Indeed, against his will, he is brought from non-being to life by some accidents... Why? He wants to know the meaning and purpose of his existence, but he is not told or he is told nonsense; he knocks—no one answers; death comes to him—also against his will. And just as people, bound by a common misfortune, feel easier when they come together in prison, so in life, you do not notice the trap when people inclined to analysis and generalizations come together and spend time exchanging proud, free ideas. In this sense, the mind is an irreplaceable pleasure."

"Absolutely right."

Without looking into his interlocutor's eyes, speaking quietly and with pauses, Andrei Yefimych continues to talk about intelligent people and conversations with them, and Mikhail Averyanych listens attentively and agrees: "Absolutely right."

"Do you not believe in the immortality of the soul?" the postmaster suddenly asks.

"No, esteemed Mikhail Averyanych, I do not believe and have no reason to believe."

"To tell you the truth, I doubt it too. Although, on the

other hand, I have this feeling, as if I will never die. Oh, I think to myself, old man, it's time to die! But there's some voice in my soul: don't believe it, you won't die!"

At the beginning of the tenth hour, Mikhail Averyanych leaves. Putting on his fur coat in the hallway, he says with a sigh:

"But fate has brought us to such a backwater! Most annoyingly, we'll have to die here. Oh!"

VII

After seeing off his friend, Andrei Yefimych sits down at the table and starts reading again. The silence of the evening and then the night is not disturbed by any sound, and time seems to stop and freeze along with the doctor over his book, and it seems that nothing exists except for this book and the lamp with its green shade. The doctor's rough, peasant-like face gradually lights up with a smile of admiration and delight at the workings of the human mind. Oh, why isn't man immortal? he thinks. Why are there brain centers and convolutions, why sight, speech, consciousness, genius, if all of this is destined to sink into the ground and eventually cool along with the earthly crust, and then for millions of years to aimlessly orbit the sun alongside the earth? To cool down and then to orbit aimlessly, it is not necessary at all to extract man from non-being with his lofty, almost divine mind and then, as if in mockery, transform him into clay.

Metabolism! But how cowardly it is to console oneself with this surrogate of immortality! Unconscious processes occurring in nature are lower even than human stupidity, because stupidity still has consciousness and will, whereas in processes there is absolutely nothing. Only a coward, who is more afraid of death than dignified, can console himself with the fact that his body will eventually live in grass, in stone, in a frog... To see one's immortality in metabolism is as strange as predicting a brilliant future for a violin case after a dear violin has shattered and become useless.

When the clock strikes, Andrei Yefimych leans back in his chair and closes his eyes to think a little. And involuntarily, under the influence of the good thoughts gleaned from the book, he casts a glance at his past and present. The past is repugnant; it's better not to think about it. And the present is the same as the past. He knows that at the time when his thoughts are orbiting along with the cooled earth around the sun, next to the doctor's apartment, people are languishing in illnesses and physical filth in a large building; perhaps someone isn't sleeping and is battling with insects, someone is getting infected with scabies or groaning from a bandage tied too tightly; perhaps the patients are playing cards with the attendants and drinking vodka. In the past year, twelve thousand people were deceived; all medical affairs, just like twenty years ago, are built on theft, scandals, gossip, nepotism, on gross charlatanism, and the hospital still remains an immoral and highly detrimental institution to the health of the residents. He knows that in Ward No. 6 behind bars, Nikita torments the patients and that Moisheika walks around the city every day collecting alms.

On the other hand, he is well aware that there has been a tremendous change in medicine over the past twenty-five years. When he was studying at university, it seemed to him that medicine would soon suffer the fate of alchemy and metaphysics, but now, as he reads at night, medicine touches him and excites in him wonder and even delight. Indeed, what an unexpected brilliance, what a revolution! Thanks to antiseptic methods, operations are performed that the great Pirogov considered impossible even in spe. Ordinary district doctors dare to perform knee joint resections, for every hundred abdominal incisions there is only one death, and kidney disease is considered such a trivial matter that it is not even written about. Syphilis is radically cured. And the theory of heredity, hypnosis, the discoveries of Pasteur and Koch, hygiene with statistics, and our Russian rural medicine? Psychiatry with its current classification of diseases, methods of diagnosis and treatment – compared to what it used to be, it's like comparing a molehill to Mount Elbrus. Now, the insane are not doused with cold water on their heads or made to wear feverish shirts; they are treated humanely and even, as newspapers report, are provided with plays and balls. Andrei Yefimych knows that with current views and tastes, such a horror as Ward No. 6 is possible perhaps only two hundred versts from the railway, in a small town where the town mayor and all the council members are semi-literate burghers who see a priest in the doctor, whom they need to believe in without any criticism, even if he pours molten lead into their mouths; whereas elsewhere, the public and newspapers would have long torn to shreds this little Bastille.

"But what then?" Andrei Yefimych asks himself, opening his eyes. "What of it all? Antiseptics, Koch, and Pasteur, and yet the essence of the matter has not changed at all. Suffering and mortality are still the same. They organize balls and plays for the mad, but still, they don't release them back into the world. So, it's all nonsense and vanity, and there is essentially no difference between the best venereal clinic and my hospital."

But sorrow and a feeling akin to envy prevent him from being indifferent. This must be from fatigue. His heavy head leans towards the book; he puts his hands under his face to make it softer, and he thinks:

"I serve a harmful cause and receive remuneration from people whom I deceive; I am dishonest. But in myself, I am nothing; I am only a particle of necessary social evil: all the district officials are harmful and receive remuneration for nothing... So, it's not me who is to blame for my dishonesty, but the times... If I were born two hundred years later, I would be different."

When three o'clock strikes, he extinguishes the lamp and goes to the bedroom. He doesn't want to sleep.

## VIII

Two years ago, the zemstvo (local government) became generous and decided to allocate three hundred rubles annually as assistance for strengthening the medical staff at the city hospital until the opening of the zemstvo hospital, and to assist Andrei Yefimych, the district doctor Evgeny Fedorych Khobotov was invited by the city. He is still very young - not yet thirty - a tall brunet with broad cheekbones and small eyes; probably his ancestors were foreigners. He arrived in the city without a penny, with a small suitcase and a young, unattractive woman whom he calls his cook. This woman has a nursing baby. Evgeny Fedorych wears a cap with a visor and high boots, and in winter he wears a fur coat. He has become close to the paramedic Sergey Sergeyich and the treasurer, but for some reason he calls the other officials aristocrats and avoids them. In his entire apartment, there is only one book - "The Latest Recipes from the Vienna Clinic for 1881". He always takes this book with him when going to see a patient. In the club, he plays billiards in the evenings but does not like cards. He enjoys using words like intricacy, manticore with vinegar, he'll cast a shadow over you, and so on, in conversation.

He visits the hospital twice a week, goes around the wards, and examines the patients. The complete absence of antiseptics and leech jars disturbs him, but he does not introduce new regulations, fearing to offend Andrei Yefimych with them. He considers his colleague, Andrei Yefimych, an old rogue, suspects him of having considerable means, and secretly envies him. He would gladly take his place.

## IX

On one of the spring evenings, at the end of March, when there was no snow on the ground anymore and the starlings were singing in the hospital garden, the doctor went out to escort his friend, the postmaster, to the gate. At that moment, the Jew Moiseyka entered the courtyard, returning from his beggary. He was without a hat, wearing small galoshes on his bare feet, and in his hands, he held a small pouch with alms.

"Give me a penny!" he addressed the doctor, trembling from the cold but smiling.

Andrei Yefimych, who never knew how to refuse, gave him a grivna.

"How unfortunate," he thought, looking at the Jew's bare feet with red, thin ankles. "They must be wet."

Driven by a feeling akin to pity and disgust, he followed the Jew into the wing, glancing at his bald patch and then at his ankles. As the doctor entered with a heap of junk, Nikita sprang up and straightened himself.

"Hello, Nikita," Andrei Yefimych said softly. "Should we give this Jew some boots, perhaps, lest he catch a cold?"

"I'm listening, your nobleman. I will inform the superintendent."

"Please do. Ask him on my behalf. Tell him I requested it."

The door from the vestibule to the ward was open. Ivan Dmitritch, lying on the bed and propped up on his elbow, anxiously listened to a stranger's voice and suddenly recognized the doctor. He shook with anger, jumped up, and with a red, angry face and wild eyes, rushed into the middle of the ward.

"The doctor has come!" he shouted and laughed. "Finally! Gentlemen, congratulations, the doctor honors us with his visit! Damn scoundrel!" he yelled and, in a fit of rage unprecedented in the ward, stamped his foot. "Kill this scoundrel! No, not just kill! Drown him in the privy!"

Andrei Yefimych, hearing this, peered into the ward from the vestibule and asked gently, "For what?"

"For what?" Ivan Dmitritch shouted, approaching him with a threatening look and nervously clutching his dressing gown. "Thief!" he said with disgust, curling his lips as if wanting to spit. "Charlatan! Hangman!"

"Calm down," said Andrei Yefimych, smiling apologetically. "I assure you, I have never stolen anything. As for the rest, you are probably greatly exaggerating. I see you are angry with me. Please calm down if you can and tell me calmly: why are you angry?"

"And why do you keep me here?"

"Because you are sick."

"Yes, I'm sick. But dozens, hundreds of lunatics roam free because your ignorance cannot distinguish them from the healthy. Why should I and these wretches sit here for everyone? You, the paramedic, the superintendent, and all your hospital scum are morally far lower than any of us. Why are we sitting here, and you're not? Where's the logic?"

"Morality and logic have nothing to do with it. It all depends on circumstance. Whoever is detained stays, and whoever isn't, walks free, that's all. There's no morality or logic in the fact that I'm a doctor and you're mentally ill, just pure chance."

"I don't understand this nonsense," Ivan Dmitritch said stupidly and sat down on his bed.

Moiseyka, whom Nikita was ashamed to search in the doctor's presence, spread pieces of bread, papers, and bones on his bed and, still trembling from the cold, began to speak rapidly and melodiously in Yiddish. He probably thought he had opened a shop.

"Let me go," said Ivan Dmitritch, his voice trembling.

"I can't."

"But why? Why?"

"Because it's not in my power. Consider, what benefit would you get if I let you go? You'll be apprehended by the townsfolk or the police and brought back here."

"Yes, yes, that's true," Ivan Dmitritch said and rubbed his forehead. "It's horrible! But what should I do? What?"

Ivan Dmitritch's voice and his young, intelligent face with grimaces appealed to Andrei Yefimych. He wanted to caress the young man and calm him down. He sat down next to him on the bed, thought for a moment, and said:

"You're asking what to do? The best thing in your situation is to run away from here. But, unfortunately, it's futile. You'll be caught. When society protects itself from criminals, mentally ill, and generally inconvenient people, it's invincible. You have only one option: to calm down and realize that your stay here is necessary."

"No one needs it."

"It doesn't matter. As long as there are prisons and asylums, someone has to be in them. If not you, then me, if not me, then someone else. Wait, when in the distant future prisons and asylums cease to exist, there won't be any bars on the windows or straitjackets. Of course, such a time will come sooner or later."

Ivan Dmitritch smiled mockingly.

"You're joking," he said, squinting. "Gentlemen like you and your assistant Nikita have no concern for the future, but rest assured, gracious sir, better times will come! Let me speak vulgarly, laugh if you will, but the dawn of a new life will shine, truth will prevail, and there will be a celebration on our street! I may not live to see it, but someone's descendants will. I welcome them from the bottom of my heart and rejoice for them! Forward! May God help you, friends!"

Ivan Dmitritch, with shining eyes, rose and, reaching out to the window, continued with excitement in his voice:

"Because of these bars, I bless you! Long live truth! I rejoice!"

"I don't find any particular reason to rejoice," said Andrei Yefimych, finding Ivan Dmitritch's gesture theatrical yet intriguing. "There will be no prisons or asylums, and truth, as you put it, will prevail. But the essence of things won't change; the laws of nature will remain the same. People will still get sick, grow old, and die just as they do now. No matter how splendid the dawn that illuminates your life, eventually, you'll be laid in a coffin and thrown into a pit."

27

"And what about immortality?"

"Eh, nonsense!"

"You don't believe it, but I do. Someone in Dostoevsky or Voltaire says that if there were no God, humans would have invented one. And I deeply believe that if there's no immortality, then the great human mind will invent it sooner or later."

"Well said," Andrei Yefimych replied, smiling with pleasure. "It's good that you believe. With such faith, one can live joyfully even bricked into a wall. Have you received an education anywhere?"

"Yes, I was at the university, but I didn't finish."

"You are a thoughtful and contemplative person. In any situation, you can find solace within yourself. Free and deep thinking, which seeks to understand life, and complete contempt for the foolishness of the world—these are two blessings higher than any known to man. And you can possess them, even if you live behind three bars. Diogenes lived in a barrel, yet he was happier than all earthly kings."

"Your Diogenes was a fool," Ivan Dmitritch said gloomily. "What are you telling me about Diogenes and understanding?," he suddenly became angry and stood up. "I love life passionately! I have a persecution complex, a constant torturous fear, but there are moments when I am seized by a thirst for life, and then I fear going mad. I terribly want to live, terribly!"

He paced the ward in agitation and said, lowering his voice:

"When I dream, ghosts visit me. People come to me, I hear voices, music, and it seems to me that I walk through some forests, along the seashore, and I long so passionately for the hustle, the bustle... Tell me, what's new there?" Ivan Dmitritch asked. "What's there?"

"Do you want to know about the city or in general?"

"Well, tell me about the city first, and then in general."

"Well then. The city is painfully dull... There's no one to talk to, no one to listen to. There are no new people.

However, a young doctor, Khobotov, recently arrived."

"He arrived while I was still there. What, a boor?"

"Yes, uncultured. It's strange, you know... Judging by everything, there's no intellectual stagnation in our capitals, there's movement—meaning there must be real people there, but for some reason, every time they send us people from there, one wouldn't look at them. Poor city!"

"Yes, a poor city!" sighed Ivan Dmitritch and laughed. "But how about in general? What are they writing in newspapers and magazines?"

It was already dark in the ward. The doctor stood up and, standing, began to talk about what they were writing abroad and in Russia and what direction of thought is now noticeable. Ivan Dmitritch listened attentively and asked questions, but suddenly, as if remembering something terrible, he grabbed his head and lay on the bed with his back to the doctor.

"What's the matter with you?" Andrei Yefimych asked.

"You won't hear another word from me!" Ivan Dmitritch said rudely. "Leave me alone!"

"Why?"

"I'm telling you, leave! What the devil?"

Andrei Yefimych shrugged, sighed, and left. Passing through the vestibule, he said:

"We should clean up here, Nikita... The smell is terribly heavy!"

"I'm listening, your nobleman!"

"What a pleasant young man!" Andrei Yefimych thought as he walked back to his apartment. "In all the time I've been here, this seems to be the first person I can really talk to. He knows how to reason and is interested in exactly what matters."

As he read and then went to bed, he kept thinking about Ivan Dmitritch, and when he woke up the next morning, he remembered that he had met an intelligent and interesting person yesterday and decided to visit him again at the first opportunity.

X

Ivan Dmitritch lay in the same position as yesterday, his head in his hands and his legs drawn up. His face was not visible.

"Hello, my friend," said Andrei Yefimych. "Are you not sleeping?"

"Firstly, you're not my friend," Ivan Dmitritch muttered into the pillow, "and secondly, you're wasting your time; you won't get a word out of me."

"Strange..." murmured Andrei Yefimych in embarrassment. "Yesterday we were talking so peacefully, but suddenly you got offended for some reason and immediately stopped... Perhaps I expressed myself awkwardly or, maybe, expressed a thought contrary to your beliefs..."

"Yes, I'll believe that!" said Ivan Dmitritch, raising himself and looking at the doctor mockingly and anxiously; his eyes were red. "You can go spy and interrogate elsewhere, there's nothing for you to do here. I understood why you came yesterday."

"Strange imagination!" chuckled the doctor. "So you think I'm a spy?"

"Yes, I do... Spy or a doctor sent to test me, it's all the same."

"Oh, you're quite the character!" The doctor sat on a stool beside the bed and shook his head reproachfully. "But let's suppose you're right," he said. "Let's suppose I'm treacherously trying to catch you out to hand you over to the police. You'll be arrested and then tried. But will it be worse for you in court and in prison than here? And if they send you to exile or even to hard labor, wouldn't that be better than sitting in this ward? I think it wouldn't be worse... So why fear?"

Apparently, these words had an effect on Ivan Dmitritch. He sat down calmly.

It was five in the evening, the time when Andrei Yefimych usually walked around his rooms and Daryushka asked him if it was time for him to drink beer. The weather outside was quiet and clear.

"I went for a walk after lunch, and here I am, as you can see," said the doctor. "Spring is here."

"What month is it now? March?" asked Ivan Dmitritch.

"Yes, end of March."

"Is it muddy outside?"

"No, not very. There are already paths in the garden."

"Now it would be nice to take a carriage ride out of town," said Ivan Dmitritch, rubbing his red eyes as if half asleep, "then come back home to a warm, cozy study and... and get treated by a decent doctor for my headache... I haven't lived like a human being for a long time. And it's nasty here! Intolerably nasty!"

After yesterday's excitement, he was tired and sluggish and spoke reluctantly. His fingers trembled, and his face showed that he had a severe headache.

"There's no difference between a warm, cozy study and this ward," said Andrei Yefimych. "A person's peace and contentment are not external but within himself."

"What do you mean?"

"An ordinary person expects good or bad from outside, that is, from the carriage and the study, but a thoughtful person expects it from himself."

"Go preach this philosophy in Greece, where it's warm and smells of oranges, but here it's not suitable. Who was it that talked about Diogenes? Was it with you?"

"Yes, yesterday with me."

"Diogenes didn't need a study or a warm room; it's already hot enough there. Just lie in your barrel and eat oranges and olives. But if he had to live in Russia, he would have requested a room not just in December, but in May as well. He'd probably have shivered from the cold."

"No. Cold, like any pain, can be unfelt. Marcus Aurelius said: 'Pain is a vivid representation of pain: make an effort of will to change this representation, dismiss it, stop complaining, and the pain will disappear.' This is true. A sage or simply a thoughtful, contemplative person is distinguished precisely by the fact that he despises suffering; he is always content and surprised by nothing."

"So, I'm an idiot because I suffer, am discontented, and am surprised by human wickedness."

"You're wrong. If you contemplate more often, you'll understand how insignificant all the external things that trouble us are. You need to strive for understanding of life, and in it lies true happiness."

"Understanding..." grimaced Ivan Dmitritch. "External, internal... Sorry, I don't understand that. I only know," he said, rising and looking angrily at the doctor, "I know that God created me from warm blood and nerves, yes! And organic tissue, if it's alive, must react to any irritation. And I react! To pain I respond with cries and tears, to wickedness with indignation, to filth with disgust. In my opinion, that's what life is, basically. The lower the organism, the less sensitive it is and the weaker its response to irritation, and the higher, the more susceptible and energetic its reaction to reality. How can one not know this? Doctor, you don't know such trivialities! To despise suffering, always be content, and be surprised by nothing, one needs to reach such a state," and Ivan Dmitritch pointed to a fat, flabby man, "or else harden oneself with suffering to such a degree as to lose all sensitivity to it, that is, in other words, to stop living. Sorry, I'm not a sage or a philosopher," Ivan Dmitritch continued irritably, "and I don't understand anything about it. I'm not capable of reasoning."

"On the contrary, you reason perfectly well."

"The Stoics, whom you're parodying, were remarkable people, but their doctrine froze two thousand years ago and hasn't budged since because it's impractical and not vital. It succeeded only with the minority, which spends its life studying and savoring various doctrines, but the majority didn't understand it. The teaching that preaches indifference to wealth, to the comforts of life, contempt for suffering and death is completely incomprehensible to the vast majority, because this majority never knew wealth or comfort in life; and to despise suffering would mean to despise life itself for it, as the whole essence of human beings consists of sensations of hunger, cold, offense, loss, and Hamlet's fear of death. In these sensations is all life: one can be burdened by it, hate it, but not despise it. Yes, repeating, the doctrine of the Stoics can never have a future, but what does progress from the beginning of the century to today is struggle, sensitivity to pain, and the ability to respond to irritation..."

Ivan Dmitritch suddenly lost his train of thought, stopped, and irritably rubbed his forehead.

"I wanted to say something important, but I got distracted," he said. "What was I saying? Ah, yes! So here's what I'm saying: one of the Stoics sold himself into slavery in order to ransom his neighbor. You see, even a Stoic reacted to irritation, because for such a generous act as sacrificing oneself for another, an indignant and compassionate soul is needed. I've forgotten everything I learned here in prison, otherwise I would have remembered something else. And what about Christ? Christ responded to reality by crying, smiling, grieving, getting angry, even feeling sorrow; he didn't smile in the face of suffering and didn't scorn death, but prayed in the Garden of Gethsemane for the cup to pass from him."

Ivan Dmitritch laughed and sat down.

"Let's suppose a person's peace and contentment are within himself," he said. "Let's suppose one should despise suffering and be surprised by nothing. But on what basis do you preach this? Are you a sage? A philosopher?"

"No, I'm not a philosopher, but everyone should preach it because it's reasonable."

"No, I want to know why you consider yourself competent in matters of understanding, contempt for suffering, and so on. Have you ever suffered? Do you have any idea what suffering is? Let me ask you: were you beaten as a child?"

"No, my parents abhorred physical punishment."

"But my father beat me severely. My father was a harsh, hemorrhoidal official, with a long nose and a yellow neck. But let's talk about you. No one laid a finger on you before your time, no one threatened or beat you; you're as healthy as a bull. You grew up under your father's wing and lived off him, then immediately snagged a sinecure. You've lived for over twenty years in a rent-free apartment, with heating, lighting, and servants, while having the right to work as much or as little as you please, even to do nothing. By nature, you're lazy and flabby, and therefore you tried to arrange your life so that nothing would bother you or move you from your place. You handed over your responsibilities to a paramedic and other scum, while you sat in warmth and silence, saved money, read books, indulged in contemplation of various lofty nonsense, and," (Ivan Dmitritch looked at the doctor's red nose) "drinking. In short, you've never seen life, you know nothing about it at all, and you're only theoretically acquainted with reality. And you despise suffering and are surprised by nothing for a very simple reason: the philosophy of vanity, external and internal contempt for life, suffering, and death, understanding, true good—all this is the most suitable philosophy for a Russian layabout. You see, for example, a man beating his wife. Why interfere? Let him beat her, they'll both die sooner or later anyway; and the one who's beating is only insulting himself with his blows, not the one he's beating. It's foolish and improper to get drunk, but to drink is to die, and not to drink is to die. A woman comes, her teeth hurt... So what? Pain is a representation of pain, and besides, you can't live in this world without illnesses; we'll all die anyway, so go away, woman, don't disturb me while I'm thinking and drinking vodka. A young man asks for advice on what to do, how to live; before answering, another person would think, but I'm ready with an answer:

strive for understanding or for true good. And what is this fantastic 'true good'? There's no answer, of course. We're kept here behind bars, tortured, tormented, but it's wonderful and reasonable because there's no difference between this ward and a warm, cozy office. Convenient philosophy: there's nothing to do, the conscience is clear, and you feel like a sage... No, sir, this is not philosophy, not thinking, not broad-mindedness, but laziness, charlatanism, sleepy stupidity... Yes!" Ivan Dmitritch got angry again. "You despise suffering, but I bet if you caught your finger in a door, you'd scream at the top of your lungs!"

"And maybe I wouldn't," said Andrei Yefimych, smiling gently.

"Yes, right! But what if you were paralyzed or, let's say, some fool and bully, taking advantage of his position and rank, publicly insulted you, and you knew he would get away with it scot-free—well, then you would understand what it means to preach to others about understanding and true good."

"That's original," said Andrei Yefimych, laughing with pleasure and rubbing his hands. "I'm pleasantly struck by your inclination for generalizations, and the characterization you've just made of me is simply brilliant. I must confess, conversing with you gives me immense pleasure. Well then, I've listened to you, now it's your turn to listen to me..."

XI

This conversation lasted for about an hour, and apparently made a deep impression on Andrei Yefimych. He started visiting the wing every day. He went there in the mornings and afternoons, and often the evening darkness found him in conversation with Ivan Dmitritch. At first, Ivan Dmitritch was suspicious of him, suspecting ill intentions, and openly expressed his dislike. But later he got used to him, and his sharp attitude changed to one of condescending irony.

Soon, rumors spread throughout the hospital that Doctor Andrei Yefimych had started visiting Ward No. 6. No one—neither the paramedic, nor Nikita, nor the nurses—could understand why he went there, why he spent hours there, what he talked about, and why he didn't prescribe any medications. His actions seemed strange. Mikhail Averyanich often didn't find him at home, something that had never happened before, and Daryushka was embarrassed because the doctor no longer drank beer at a set time and sometimes even arrived late for lunch.

Once, it was already the end of June, Doctor Khobotov came to see Andrei Yefimych on some business; not finding him at home, he went to look for him in the courtyard; there he was told that the old doctor had gone to the mental patients. Entering the wing and stopping in the vestibule, Khobotov overheard the following conversation:

"We will never agree, and you won't be able to convert me to your faith," Ivan Dmitritch said irritably. "You are completely unfamiliar with reality, and you have never suffered, you only, like a drunkard, fed off others' sufferings, while I have suffered continuously from the day I was born until today. So, I say frankly: I consider myself superior to you and more competent in all respects. You have no right to teach me."

"I have no intention of converting you to my faith at all," Andrei Yefimych said quietly and regretfully, feeling misunderstood. "And that's not the point, my friend. It's not about you suffering and me not. Suffering and joys are transient; let's leave them, God be with them. The point is that you and I think; we see each other as people capable of thinking and reasoning, and that makes us united, no matter how different our views may be. If you only knew, my friend, how tired I am of universal madness, incompetence, stupidity, and how much joy I feel every time I talk to you! You are an intelligent person, and I enjoy your company."

Khobotov opened the door a crack and glanced into the ward; Ivan Dmitritch in his cap and Doctor Andrei

Yefimych sat side by side on the bed. The madman grimaced, twitched, and convulsively clutched his robe, while the doctor sat motionless, his head bowed, his face red, helpless, and sad. Khobotov shrugged, smiled, and exchanged glances with Nikita. Nikita shrugged too.

The next day, Khobotov came to the wing together with the paramedic. Both stood in the vestibule and eavesdropped.

"Our old man seems to have completely lost it!" Khobotov said, coming out of the wing.

"Lord, have mercy on us sinners!" sighed the distinguished Sergey Sergeyich, carefully avoiding puddles so as not to soil his brightly polished boots. "To tell you the truth, dear Yevgeny Fedorych, I've been expecting this for a long time!"

## XII

After this, Andrei Yefimych began to notice a certain mystery surrounding him. Men, nurses, and patients, upon meeting him, would look at him questioningly and then whisper among themselves. The girl Masha, the caretaker's daughter whom he used to enjoy meeting in the hospital garden, now, when he approached her with a smile to pat her on the head, for some reason ran away from him. Postmaster Mikhail Averyanich, while listening to him, no longer said, "Absolutely right," but mumbled in incomprehensible embarrassment, "Yes, yes, yes..." and looked at him thoughtfully and sadly. For some reason, he began advising his friend to give up vodka and beer, but as a delicate person, he spoke indirectly, hinting, telling stories about a battalion commander, a fine man, or about a regimental priest, a splendid fellow, who drank and fell ill but, after quitting drinking, completely recovered. Two or three times, Andrei Yefimych's colleague Khobotov came to him; he also advised giving up alcoholic drinks and recommended taking potassium bromide without any apparent reason.

In August, Andrei Yefimych received a letter from the city mayor asking him to come for a very important matter. Arriving at the appointed time at the city hall, Andrei Yefimych found there the military chief, the resident caretaker of the district school, a member of the city council, Khobotov, and another gentleman, a tall blond man, who was introduced to him as a doctor. This doctor, with a Polish surname that was difficult to pronounce, lived thirty versts from the city, at a stud farm, and was passing through the city.

"So, there's a matter at hand concerning your part," the council member addressed Andrei Yefimych after everyone had greeted each other and sat down at the table. "Here, Yevgeny Fedorych says that the pharmacy is a bit cramped in the main building and that it should be moved to one of the wings. Of course, that's fine, it can be moved, but the main reason is that the wing will need repairs."

"Yes, it can't do without repairs," Andrei Yefimych said, pondering. "For example, if we were to adapt one of the corner wings for the pharmacy, I estimate it would require a minimum of five hundred rubles. The expenditure would be unproductive."

They fell silent for a moment.

"I had the honor of reporting ten years ago," Andrei Yefimych continued in a quiet voice, "that this hospital in its current state is a luxury for the city beyond its means. It was built in the forties, but at that time, the means were not as sufficient. The city spends too much on unnecessary buildings and redundant positions. I think with this money, under different arrangements, we could maintain two exemplary hospitals."

"So let's introduce different arrangements!" the council member briskly said.

"I've already had the honor of reporting: transfer the medical part to the jurisdiction of the zemstvo."

"Yes, give the money to the zemstvo, and it will

embezzle it," chuckled the blond doctor.

"That's how it goes," agreed the council member, laughing too.

Andrei Yefimych looked weakly and dimly at the blond doctor and said, "We must be fair."

They fell silent again. Tea was served. The military chief, for some reason very embarrassed, reached across the table to touch Andrei Yefimych's hand and said:

"You've completely forgotten about us, Doctor. But then, you're like a monk: you don't play cards, you don't love women. You're bored with our brother."

Everyone started talking about how boring it is for a decent person to live in this city. No theater, no music, and at the last dance evening at the club, there were about twenty ladies and only two gentlemen. The youth doesn't dance; they just crowd around the buffet or play cards all the time. Andrei Yefimych slowly and quietly, without looking at anyone, began to talk about how regrettable it is, how deeply regrettable it is, that the townspeople waste their life energy, their heart, and mind on cards and gossip, instead of knowing how to and wanting to spend time in interesting conversation and reading, not wanting to enjoy the pleasures that intellect offers. Only one intellect is interesting and remarkable; everything else is petty and lowly. Khobotov listened attentively to his colleague and suddenly asked:

"Andrei Yefimych, what's the date today?"

After receiving the answer, he and the blond doctor, with the tone of examiners feeling their incompetence, began to ask Andrei Yefimych what day it was, how many days are in a year, and if it's true that there is a remarkable prophet living in Ward No. 6.

In response to the last question, Andrei Yefimych blushed and said, "Yes, he's a patient, but an interesting young man."

They didn't ask him any more questions.

That evening, Mikhail Averyanich visited him. Without

greeting, the postmaster approached him, took both his hands, and said in an excited voice:

"My dear, my friend, prove to me that you believe in my sincere disposition and consider me your friend... My friend!" And, interrupting Andrei Yefimych, he continued, agitatedly: "I love you for your education and noble soul. Listen to me, my dear. The rules of science require doctors to hide the truth from you, but I'm cutting straight to the truth like a soldier: you're unwell! Forgive me, my dear, but it's true, everyone around has noticed it long ago. Just now, Doctor Yevgeny Fedorych told me that for the sake of your health, you need to rest and have some fun. Absolutely right! Excellent! In a few days, I'm taking leave and going away for a change of air. Prove that you're my friend, let's go together! Let's go, shake off the old days."

"I feel perfectly healthy," said Andrei Yefimych, thinking. "But I can't go. Allow me to prove my friendship to you in some other way."

To go somewhere, for unknown reasons, without books, without Daryushka, without beer, to abruptly disrupt the order of life established over twenty years - such an idea seemed wild and fantastical to him at first. But he remembered the conversation that had taken place at the city hall, and the heavy mood he had felt on the way home from the city hall, and the thought of leaving the city for a short time, where foolish people considered him insane, smiled at him.

"And where exactly do you intend to go?" he asked.

"To Moscow, to St. Petersburg, to Warsaw... In Warsaw, I spent the happiest five years of my life. What an amazing city! Come with me, my dear!"

XIII

A week later, Andrey Efimych was offered a break, that is, to retire, to which he reacted indifferently, and another week later, he and Mikhail Averyanich were already sitting in a postal tarantas and heading to the nearest railway station. The days were cool, clear, with a blue sky and transparent distance. They covered two hundred versts to the station in two days and spent two nights along the way. When they were served poorly washed glasses for tea at the postal stations or the horses were hitched for a long time, Mikhail Averyanich turned purple, shook all over, and shouted, "Silence! No reasoning!" And sitting in the tarantas, he kept talking about his travels in the Caucasus and the Kingdom of Poland without stopping for a minute. There were so many adventures, what encounters! He spoke loudly and at the same time made such surprised eyes that one could think he was lying. Moreover, as he spoke, he breathed into Andrey Efimych's face and laughed loudly in his ear. This embarrassed the doctor and prevented him from thinking and concentrating.

They traveled by third class on the train, in the non-smoking carriage. The public was half clean. Mikhail Averyanich soon got acquainted with everyone and, moving from bench to bench, loudly said that one should not travel on these outrageous roads. Fraud all around! It's different riding on horseback: you can cover a hundred versts in a day and then feel healthy and fresh. Our crops fail because we drained the Pinsk swamps. Generally, there is terrible disorder. He got heated, spoke loudly, and didn't let others speak. This endless chatter interspersed with loud laughter and expressive gestures tired Andrey Efimych.

"Which of us is crazy?" he thought with annoyance. "Is it me, who tries not to disturb the passengers in any way, or this egotist who thinks he's smarter and more interesting than everyone else here, and therefore won't let anyone rest?"

In Moscow, Mikhail Averyanich put on a military frock coat without epaulets and trousers with red stripes. On the street, he walked in a military cap and an overcoat, and the soldiers saluted him. Andrey Efimych now felt that this was a man who had squandered all the good things from his master's estate, leaving only the bad. He liked to be served, even when it was completely unnecessary. Matches lay on the table in front of him, and he saw them, but he shouted at the man to bring him matches; in front of the chambermaid, he didn't hesitate to walk around in just his underwear; he addressed all the servants indiscriminately, even the elderly, informally, and, when angry, called them blockheads and fools. This, as it seemed to Andrey Efimych, was aristocratic but distasteful.

First of all, Mikhail Averyanich took his friend to the Iveron Icon. He prayed fervently, with prostrations and tears, and when he finished, he sighed deeply and said:

"Even if you don't believe, it's somehow more peaceful when you pray. Come on, my dear."

Andrey Efimych was embarrassed and leaned toward the icon, while Mikhail Averyanich pursed his lips, shook his head, prayed softly, and tears welled up in his eyes again. Then they went to the Kremlin and looked at the Tsar Cannon and Tsar Bell there, and even touched them with their fingers, admired the view of Zamoskvorechye, visited the Cathedral of Christ the Savior and the Rumyantsev Museum.

They had lunch at Testov's. Mikhail Averyanich looked at the menu for a long time, smoothing the lapels, and said in the tone of a gourmet who is used to feeling at home in restaurants:

"Let's see what you're going to feed us with today, my angel!"

## XIV

The doctor walked, looked, ate, drank, but he felt one thing: annoyance at Mikhail Averyanich. He wanted to get away from his friend, to hide, but his friend considered it his duty not to let him out of his sight for a moment and to provide him with as much entertainment as possible. When there was nothing to see, he entertained him with conversations. Andrey Efimych endured it for two days, but on the third, he announced to his friend that he was sick and wanted to stay home all day. His friend said that in that case, he would stay too. Indeed, one needed rest, otherwise one would run out of steam. Andrey Efimych lay on the sofa, facing the back, and gritted his teeth, listening to his friend, who passionately assured him that France would sooner or later crush Germany, that Moscow had a lot of fraudsters, and that one couldn't judge a horse's merits by its appearance. The doctor's ears started buzzing, and his heart raced, but out of delicacy, he didn't dare ask his friend to leave or to be silent. Fortunately, Mikhail Averyanich got bored of staying in the room, and after lunch, he went out for a walk.

Alone at last, Andrey Efimych surrendered to the feeling of rest. How pleasant it was to lie still on the sofa and realize that you were alone in the room! True happiness is impossible without solitude. The fallen angel must have changed his mind about God, probably because he desired solitude, which angels do not know. Andrey Efimych wanted to think about what he had seen and heard in the past few days, but Mikhail Averyanich wouldn't leave his mind.

"He took leave and came with me out of friendship, out of generosity," the doctor thought with annoyance. "There's nothing worse than this friendly care. Here he seems kind, generous, and jolly, but he's dull. Intolerably dull. There are people who always speak only wise and good words, but you feel that they are stupid people."

In the following days, Andrey Efimych claimed to be ill and didn't leave his room. He lay facing the back of the sofa and suffered when his friend entertained him with conversations or rested when his friend was absent. He was annoyed with himself for going, and with his friend, who became more talkative and relaxed with each passing day; he couldn't seem to set his thoughts on a serious, elevated tone.

"This is the reality that Ivan Dmitrievich spoke of," he thought, angry at his pettiness. "Well, nonsense... I'll come home, and everything will go back to normal..."

And in St. Petersburg, it was the same: he didn't leave his room for entire days, lying on the sofa and only getting up to have a beer.

Mikhail Averyanich kept urging to go to Warsaw all the time.

"My dear, why should I go there?" Andrey Efimych pleaded. "Go by yourself, and let me go home! I beg you!"

"Not under any circumstances!" protested Mikhail Averyanich. "It's an amazing city. I spent the happiest five years of my life there."

Andrey Efimych didn't have the strength of character to insist on his own way, and he reluctantly went to Warsaw. There he stayed in his room, lying on the sofa and seething with anger at himself, his friend, and the servants who stubbornly refused to understand Russian, while Mikhail Averyanich, as usual, healthy, lively, and cheerful, strolled around the city from morning till night, seeking out his old acquaintances. Several times he didn't come home for the night. After one such night spent goodness knows where, he returned home early in the morning in a highly excited state, red and disheveled. He paced back and forth for a long time, muttering something to himself, then stopped and said:

"Honor above all else!"

After pacing a little more, he grabbed his head and said in a tragic voice:

"Yes, honor above all else! Cursed be the moment I first thought of going to this Babylon! My dear," he turned to the doctor, "despise me: I've lost! Give me five hundred rubles!"

Andrey Efimych counted out five hundred rubles in silence and handed them to his friend. Still flushed with shame and anger, he muttered some unnecessary oath, put on his cap, and left. Returning two hours later, he collapsed into a chair, sighed loudly, and said:

"Honor is saved! Let's go, my friend! I don't want to

spend a single minute more in this cursed city. Fraudsters! Austrian spies!"

When the friends returned to their own city, it was already November, and deep snow lay on the streets. Dr. Hobotov took Andrey Efimych's place; he still lived in the old apartment, waiting for Andrey Efimych to return and clean up the hospital apartment. The unattractive woman whom he called his cook was already living in one of the wings.

New hospital gossip circulated around the city. It was said that the unattractive woman had quarreled with the superintendent, and he was supposedly crawling on his knees before her, begging for forgiveness.

On the first day of his return, Andrey Efimych had to find himself an apartment.

"My friend," the postmaster said to him timidly, "forgive me for the intrusive question: what means do you have at your disposal?"

Andrey Efimych silently counted his money and said:

"Eighty-six rubles."

"I'm not asking about that," Mikhail Averyanich said, embarrassed, not understanding the doctor. "I'm asking about your means in general?"

"I'm telling you: eighty-six rubles... I have nothing more."

Mikhail Averyanich considered the doctor an honest and noble man, but still suspected that he had some capital, at least twenty thousand. Now, learning that Andrey Efimych was penniless, that he had nothing to live on, he suddenly burst into tears and hugged his friend.

XV

Andrey Efimych lived in a three-windowed house of the bourgeois Belova. In this house, there were only three rooms, not counting the kitchen. The doctor occupied two of them, with windows facing the street, while the third

45

room and the kitchen were inhabited by Daryushka and the bourgeois with their three children. Sometimes, the landlady's lover, a drunken man, came to spend the night, raging at night and terrifying the children and Daryushka. When he arrived and, seating himself in the kitchen, began demanding vodka, everyone felt very cramped, and out of pity, the doctor took the crying children and laid them on the floor in his own room, which gave him great pleasure.

He still rose at eight o'clock and after tea sat down to read his old books and magazines. There was no money left for new ones. Perhaps because the books were old, or maybe because a change of environment no longer captivated him deeply and tired him. To avoid idleness, he compiled a detailed catalog of his books and attached tickets to their spines, and this mechanical, painstaking work seemed more interesting to him than reading. Monotonous, painstaking work somehow lulled his thoughts; he thought of nothing, and time passed quickly. Even sitting in the kitchen and peeling potatoes with Daryushka or picking out impurities from buckwheat seemed interesting to him. On Saturdays and Sundays, he went to church. Standing near the wall and closing his eyes, he listened to the singing and thought about his father, his mother, the university, about religions; he felt calm, sad, and then, leaving the church, he regretted that the service ended so soon.

He went to the hospital to see Ivan Dmitrich twice to talk to him. But both times Ivan Dmitrich was unusually agitated and angry; he asked to be left alone, as he was tired of empty talk, and said that for all his suffering, he asked for only one reward - solitary confinement. Are they even denying him that? When Andrey Efimych said goodbye to him both times and wished him goodnight, he grumbled and said:

"To hell with it!"

And Andrey Efimych now didn't know whether to go to him a third time or not. But he wanted to go.

Before, in the afternoons, Andrey Efimych used to walk

around the rooms and think, but now from after lunch until evening tea, he lay on the sofa facing the back and surrendered to petty thoughts that he couldn't overcome. He was offended that over his more than twenty years of service, he had not been given a pension or a one-time allowance. True, he hadn't served honestly, but all civil servants receive a pension regardless of whether they are honest or not. Modern justice lies precisely in the fact that ranks, orders, and pensions are awarded not for moral qualities and abilities, but for service, whatever it may be. Why then should he be an exception? He had no money at all. He felt ashamed to pass by the shop and look at the landlady. Thirty-two rubles were already owed for beer. Belova owed money too. Daryushka was slowly selling old clothes and books and lied to the landlady, saying that the doctor would soon receive a lot of money.

He was angry with himself for spending a thousand rubles on the trip, which he had saved up. How useful that thousand would be now! He was annoyed that people didn't leave him alone. Hobotov considered it his duty to occasionally visit his sick colleague. Everything about him disgusted Andrey Efimych: his well-fed face, his bad, condescending tone, the word "colleague," and his high boots; but the most disgusting thing was that he considered it his duty to treat Andrey Efimych and thought that he was really treating him. At each visit, he brought a glass with potassium bromide and pills made from rhubarb.

And Mikhail Averyanich also considered it his duty to visit his friend and entertain him. Every time he entered Andrey Efimych's place with affected carelessness, forced laughter, and began to assure him that he looked great today and that things, thank God, were getting better, and from this, one could conclude that he considered his friend's situation hopeless. He hadn't yet paid off his Warsaw debt and was weighed down by heavy shame, was tense, and therefore tried to laugh louder and tell funnier stories. His anecdotes and stories now seemed endless and were painful for both Andrey Efimych and himself.

In his presence, Andrey Efimych usually lay on the sofa facing the wall and listened, gritting his teeth; a sediment settled on his soul, and after each visit from his friend, he felt that sediment rising higher and seemed to reach his throat.

To drown out petty feelings, he hastened to think about how he, Hobotov, and Mikhail Averyanich must eventually perish, leaving no trace in nature. If one were to imagine that in a million years, some spirit would pass by the earth in space, it would see only clay and bare rocks. Everything - culture, moral law - would disappear and not even grow as much as a burdock. What did the shame in front of the shopkeeper, the insignificant Hobotov, the heavy friendship of Mikhail Averyanich mean? It was all nonsense and trivialities.

But such reasoning no longer helped. As soon as he imagined the earth in a million years, Hobotov in high boots or Mikhail Averyanich laughing loudly would appear from behind the bare rock, and he even heard a timid whisper: "And the Warsaw debt, darling, I'll repay it one of these days... Definitely."

XVI

Once, after lunch, Mikhail Averyanych arrived while Andrey Efimych was lying on the sofa. It so happened that at the same time, Hobotov arrived with potassium bromide. Andrey Efimych struggled to sit up, leaning on the sofa with both hands.

"Well, my dear," began Mikhail Averyanich, "today your complexion is much better than yesterday. You're doing great! By God, you're doing great!"

"It's time, time to recover, colleague," said Hobotov, yawning. "I bet you're tired of all this nonsense."

"And we'll recover!" cheerfully exclaimed Mikhail Averyanych. "We'll live for another hundred years! That's right!"

"A hundred or not, twenty more will do," consoled Hobotov. "Don't worry, colleague... Things will get better."

"We'll still show ourselves!" Mikhail Averyanych laughed and patted his friend's knee. "We'll show them! Next summer, God willing, we'll go to the Caucasus and ride all over it - yee-haw! And when we return from the Caucasus, we might as well celebrate a wedding. - Mikhail Averyanych winked slyly. - We'll marry you off, dear friend... we'll marry..."

Andrey Efimych suddenly felt the sediment rising in his throat; his heart pounded heavily.

"This is outrageous!" he said, quickly standing up and stepping back to the window. "Don't you realize you're talking nonsense?"

He wanted to continue gently and politely, but against his will, he clenched his fists and raised them above his head.

"Leave me alone!" he shouted in a voice not his own, turning crimson and trembling all over. "Get out! Both of you, get out!"

Mikhail Averyanych and Hobotov stood up and stared at him first with bewilderment, then with fear.

"Both of you, get out!" Andrey Efimych continued to shout. "Stupid people! Foolish people! I don't need your friendship or your medicines, you stupid man! It's all nonsense!"

Hobotov and Mikhail Averyanych, exchanging confused glances, retreated to the door and left for the hallway. Andrey Efimych grabbed the glass with potassium bromide and threw it after them; the glass shattered against the threshold with a clang.

"Get out of here to hell!" he shouted with a tearful voice, running into the hallway. "To hell with you!"

After the guests left, Andrey Efimych, trembling as if in a fever, lay down on the sofa and repeated for a long time:

"Stupid people! Foolish people!"

When he calmed down, his first thought was that poor

Mikhail Averyanych must now be terribly ashamed and burdened, and that all this was awful. Nothing like this had ever happened before. Where was the intelligence and tact? Where was the understanding of things and philosophical indifference?

The doctor couldn't sleep all night from shame and regret for himself, and in the morning, around ten o'clock, he went to the post office and apologized to the postmaster.

"Let's not dwell on what happened," sighed the touched Mikhail Averyanych, shaking his hand warmly. "Let bygones be bygones. Lyubavkin!" he suddenly shouted so loudly that all the postmen and visitors flinched. "Bring a chair. And you wait!" he shouted at the woman who was handing him a registered letter through the grille. "Can't you see I'm busy? Let's not dwell on the past," he continued gently, addressing Andrey Efimych. "Please, sit down, my dear."

He stroked his knees in silence for a minute and then said:

"I never intended to offend you. Illness is no joke, I understand. Your seizure scared both the doctor and me yesterday, and we talked about you for a long time afterward. My dear friend, why don't you want to take your illness seriously? How can you live like this? Excuse my frankness," Mikhail Averyanych whispered, "you're living in the most unfavorable conditions: cramped, unclean, no one to take care of you, no means for treatment... My dear friend, with all our hearts, the doctor and I implore you to listen to our advice: go to the hospital! There you'll get healthy food, care, and treatment. Evgeny Fedorych, though a bit of a formalist, between us, but knowledgeable, you can rely on him completely. He promised me he'll take care of you."

Andrey Efimych was touched by the sincere concern and tears that suddenly appeared on the postmaster's cheeks.

"Dear, don't believe them!" he whispered, putting his hand on his heart. "Don't believe them! It's a trick! My illness is only that for twenty years I've found in the whole city only one intelligent person, and he's insane. There's no illness at all, I just got caught in a vicious circle with no way out. I don't care, I'm ready for anything."

"Go to the hospital, my dear."

"I don't care, even if it's a grave."

"Promise me, darling, that you'll listen to everything Evgeny Fedorych says."

"Very well, I promise. But, I repeat, dear, I'm caught in a vicious circle. Now everything, even the sincere concern of my friends, tends toward one thing - my demise. I'm perishing and have the courage to admit it."

"Darling, you'll recover."

"Why say that?" Andrey Efimych said irritably. "Rare is the person who at the end of life doesn't feel what I feel now. When they tell you that you have something like bad kidneys and an enlarged heart, and you start treating yourself, or they tell you you're crazy or a criminal, in short, when people suddenly pay attention to you, know that you've fallen into a vicious circle from which there's no escape. You'll try to get out and get even more lost. Give up, because no human effort will save you now. That's what I think."

Meanwhile, a crowd had gathered at the grille. Andrey Efimych, not wanting to interfere, stood up and began to bid farewell. Mikhail Averyanych took his honest word once again and escorted him to the outer door.

On the same day, before evening, Hobotov unexpectedly came to Andrey Efimych in a fur coat and high boots and said in a tone as if nothing had happened yesterday:

"I've come to you on business, colleague. I've come to invite you: wouldn't you like to accompany me to a medical conference?"

Thinking that Hobotov wanted to entertain him with a walk or indeed give him a chance to earn some money, Andrey Efimych got dressed and went out with him onto the street. He was glad for the opportunity to make amends for yesterday's guilt and reconciled in his heart, thanking

Hobotov, who didn't even mention yesterday's incident and apparently spared him. It was hard to expect such delicacy from such an uncultured person.

"Where's your patient?" asked Andrey Efimych.

"He's in my hospital. I've long wanted to show you... a very interesting case."

They entered the hospital yard and, bypassing the main building, headed to the wing where the mentally ill were housed. And all this for some reason in silence. When they entered the wing, Nikita, as usual, jumped up and stretched.

"One of them had a lung complication," Hobotov said in a half-whisper, entering the ward with Andrey Efimych. "Stay here, and I'll be right back. Just need to get a stethoscope."

And he left.

XVII

It was getting dark. Ivan Dmitrievich lay on his bed, burying his face in the pillow; the paralytic sat still, quietly crying and moving his lips. The fat man and the former sorter were asleep. It was quiet.

Andrey Efimych sat on Ivan Dmitrievich's bed and waited. But half an hour passed, and instead of Hobotov, Nikita entered the ward, holding a bundle of robes, someone's laundry, and shoes.

"Please get dressed, Your Excellency," he said softly. "Here's your bed, please come here," he added, pointing to the empty bed, obviously recently brought in. "Don't worry, God willing, you'll recover."

Andrey Efimych understood everything. Without saying a word, he moved to the bed indicated by Nikita and sat down; seeing that Nikita was standing and waiting, he undressed completely, feeling ashamed. Then he put on the hospital gown; the trousers were very short, the shirt was long, and the gown smelled of smoked fish.

"You'll recover, God willing," Nikita repeated.

He took Andrey Efimych's clothes in the bundle, walked out, and closed the door behind him.

"All the same..." thought Andrey Efimych, shamefully putting on the gown and feeling like a prisoner in his new attire. "All the same... Whether it's a tailcoat, a uniform, or this gown..."

But what about the watch? And the notebook in the side pocket? And the cigarettes? Where did Nikita take the clothes? Perhaps now, until the end of his days, he wouldn't have to put on trousers, a waistcoat, and boots. All of this seemed strange and even incomprehensible at first. Andrey Efimych was still convinced that there was no difference between the house of the merchant Belova and Ward No. 6, that everything in this world was nonsense and vanity, yet his hands trembled, his legs grew cold, and he felt terrified at the thought that soon Ivan Dmitrievich would get up and see him in the gown. He got up, paced around, and sat back down.

He had been sitting like this for half an hour, an hour, and he was bored to tears; could one really live here for a day, a week, or even years, like these people? Well, here he was sitting, he got up and walked around, sat back down; could one just go and look out the window and then walk from corner to corner again? And then what? Sit like a statue all the time and think? No, that was hardly possible.

Andrey Efimych lay down, but immediately got up, wiped the cold sweat from his forehead with his sleeve, and felt that his whole face smelled of smoked fish. He paced around again.

"This is some misunderstanding..." he muttered, spreading his arms in bewilderment. "I need to explain, there's a misunderstanding here..."

At this time, Ivan Dmitrievich woke up. He sat up and rested his cheeks on his fists. He spat. Then he lazily looked at the doctor and apparently didn't understand anything at first; but soon his sleepy face turned angry and mocking.

"Ah, they put you in here too, darling!" he said with a

hoarse, half-asleep voice, squinting one eye. "Very glad. You used to suck people's blood, and now they'll suck it out of you. Excellent!"

"This is some misunderstanding..." Andrey Efimych muttered, alarmed by Ivan Dmitrievich's words; he shrugged and repeated, "Some kind of misunderstanding..."

Ivan Dmitrievich spat again and lay down.

"Damn life!" he grumbled. "And how bitter and offensive it is, because this life will end not with a reward for suffering, not with an apotheosis, like in an opera, but with death; men will come and drag the dead one by the hands and feet into the basement. Brr! Well, never mind... But there will be a celebration for us in the afterlife... I'll come from the other world as a shadow and scare these bastards. I'll make them turn gray."

Moiseyka returned and, seeing the doctor, reached out his hand.

"Give me a kopeck!" he said.

## XVIII

Andrey Efimych stepped away from the window and looked out into the field. It was already dark, and on the horizon to the right, a cold, crimson moon was rising. Not far from the hospital fence, about a hundred yards away, stood a tall white building surrounded by a stone wall. It was a prison.

"So this is reality!" thought Andrey Efimych, and he felt afraid.

The moon, the prison, the nails on the fence, and the distant flame at the brick factory were all terrifying. A sigh came from behind. Andrey Efimych turned around and saw a man with shining stars and medals on his chest, who was smiling and winking slyly. And that seemed terrifying.

Andrey Efimych reassured himself that there was nothing special about the moon and the prison, that mentally healthy people also wore medals, and that everything would eventually fade away and turn to dust, but despair suddenly seized him. He grabbed the bars with both hands and shook them with all his might. The sturdy bars didn't budge.

Then, to ease his fear, he went to Ivan Dmitrievich's bed and sat down.

"I've lost heart, my dear," he murmured, trembling and wiping cold sweat. "Lost heart."

"And you philosophize," Ivan Dmitrievich said mockingly.

"Oh my God, oh my God... Yes, yes... You once deigned to say that there's no philosophy in Russia, but everyone philosophizes, even the riffraff. But what harm does the riffraff's philosophizing do to anyone?" Andrey Efimych said in a tone as if he wanted to cry and lament. "Why, my dear, this malicious laughter? And how can one not philosophize when the riffraff is dissatisfied? To an intelligent, educated, proud, freedom-loving person, a semblance of God, there is no other way but to become a doctor in a dirty, stupid little town, and spend his whole life with jars, leeches, and mustard plasters! Quackery, narrow-mindedness, vulgarity! Oh my God!"

"You're talking nonsense. If you find being a doctor repulsive, you should have become a minister," Ivan Dmitrievich retorted.

"Nowhere, nowhere can we go. We are weak, my dear... I was indifferent, reasoned boldly and healthily, but as soon as life roughly touched me, I lost heart... prostration... We are weak, miserable... And you too, my dear. You're intelligent, noble, with the goodness of your mother's milk, but as soon as you entered life, you grew tired and fell ill... Weak, weak!"

Something else besides fear and a sense of offense tormented Andrey Efimych all evening. Finally, he realized that he wanted beer and cigarettes.

"I'll leave here, my dear," he said. "I'll ask them to bring some fire here... I can't... I'm not able to..."

Andrey Efimych went to the door and opened it, but immediately Nikita jumped up and blocked his way.

"Where are you going? You can't, you can't! It's time to sleep!" he said.

"But just for a minute, to walk in the courtyard!" Andrey Efimych stammered.

"You can't, you can't, it's not allowed. You know yourself."

Nikita closed the door and leaned against it with his back.

"But if I leave here, what harm will it do to anyone?" Andrey Efimych shrugged. "I don't understand! Nikita, I must go out!" he said, his voice trembling. "I need to!"

"Don't start trouble, it's not good!" Nikita said instructively.

"It's damn what it is!" suddenly exclaimed Ivan Dmitrievich, jumping up. "What right does he have not to let us out? How dare they keep us here? The law clearly states that no one can be deprived of freedom without trial! It's violence! Tyranny!"

"Of course, tyranny!" Andrey Efimych echoed, encouraged by Ivan Dmitrievich's outcry. "I need to, I must go out. He has no right! Let go, I'm telling you!"

"Do you hear, you dumb brute?" Ivan Dmitrievich shouted and pounded on the door. "Open up, or I'll break the door down! Murderer!"

Nikita quickly opened the door, roughly pushed Andrey Efimych aside with both hands and a knee, then swung and punched him in the face. Andrey Efimych felt as if a huge salty wave had engulfed him and dragged him to the bed; indeed, there was a salty taste in his mouth: probably blood from his teeth. As if wanting to resurface, he waved his arms and grabbed someone's bed, and at that moment felt Nikita hit him twice in the back.

Ivan Dmitrievich screamed loudly. They must have been hitting him too.

Then everything fell silent. The liquid moonlight filtered through the bars, and a shadow lay on the floor, resembling a net. It was terrifying. Andrey Efimych lay down and held his breath; he waited with horror for another blow. It felt as if someone had taken a sickle, thrust it into him, and turned it several times in his chest and guts. From the pain, he bit the pillow and clenched his teeth, and suddenly amidst the chaos, a terrible, unbearable thought flashed through his mind: that these same people, who now seemed like black shadows in the moonlight, must have felt the same pain day after day, year after year. How could it have happened that for more than twenty years he didn't know or didn't want to know about it? He didn't know, had no concept of pain, so he wasn't guilty, but conscience, just as unyielding and rude as Nikita, made him shiver from head to toe. He jumped up, wanted to shout as loud as he could and run away to kill Nikita, then Hobotov, the overseer, and the field nurse, then himself, but not a single sound came from his chest, and his legs wouldn't obey; gasping, he tore off his gown and shirt, tore them, and fell unconscious on the bed.

XIX

The next morning, he had a headache, ringing in his ears, and felt unwell all over his body. He felt no shame in remembering his weakness from yesterday. He had been timid yesterday, even afraid of the moon, sincerely expressing feelings and thoughts he hadn't realized he had before. For example, thoughts about the dissatisfaction of the philosophizing riffraff. But now he didn't care.

He didn't eat, didn't drink, lay still, and remained silent.

"I don't care," he thought when asked questions. "I won't answer... I don't care."

After lunch, Mikhail Averyanich came and brought a quarter of tea and a pound of marmalade. Daryushka also came and stood by his bed for a whole hour with a look of dull sorrow on her face. Dr. Hobotov also visited him. He brought a glass with bromide potassium and ordered Nikita to smoke something in the ward.

In the evening, Andrey Efimych died of a stroke. At first, he felt a staggering chill and nausea; something disgusting seemed to penetrate his entire body, even his fingers, pulling from his stomach to his head and flooding his eyes and ears. His vision turned green. Andrey Efimych realized it was the end for him, and he remembered that Ivan Dmitrievich, Mikhail Averyanich, and millions of people believed in immortality. But he didn't want immortality, and he thought about it only for a moment. A herd of deer, extraordinarily beautiful and graceful, which he had read about yesterday, ran past him; then a woman handed him a registered letter... Mikhail Averyanich said something. Then everything disappeared, and Andrey Efimych was lost forever.

Men came, took him by the arms and legs, and carried him to the chapel. There he lay on the table with his eyes open, illuminated by the moon at night. In the morning, Sergey Sergeyich came, devoutly prayed at the crucifix, and closed the eyes of his former boss.

Two days later, Andrey Efimych was buried. The only ones at the funeral were Mikhail Averyanich and Daryushka.

1892

Printed in Great Britain
by Amazon

46236470R00036